MW00933936

stories from india

under the banyan

Eyes on the Peacock's Tail *a folktale from Rajasthan*
Magic Vessels *a folktale from Tamilnadu*
Hiss, Don't Bite! *a folktale from Bengal*
A Curly Tale *a folktale from Bihar*
All Free *a folktale from Gujarat*
Mazzoo Mazzoo *a folktale from Kashmir*
Wrestling Mania *a folktale from Punjab*
Sweet and Salty *a folktale from Andhra Pradesh*

Wrestling Mania (English)
ISBN 978-81-86838-77-8
© & ℗ 2002 Karadi Tales Company Pvt. Ltd.

First published in India, 2003
Reprinted in 2005, 2009, 2011

Produced by
Karadi Tales Company Pvt. Ltd., PO Box 8732, Adyar, Chennai 600 020, India
phone 91 44 4421775 *fax* 91 44 4422443 *email* karadi2000@vsnl.com

Published by
Tulika Publishers, 13 Prithvi Avenue First Street, Abhiramapuram, Chennai 600 018, India
email tulikabooks@vsnl.com *website* www.tulikabooks.com

Printed and bound by
Shree Balaji Printers Pvt. Ltd, 82/2A Kamaraj Salai, Virugambakkam, Chennai 600 092, India

To order books visit www.tulikabooks.com

a folktale from punjab

Wrestling Mania

by Sandhya Rao
art by Srividya Natarajan

Tarlochan was the best wrestler this side of the Sutlej river. He had tested his strength with everyone and was actually quite bored of defeating the same people all the time. He longed for something different, some action.

"It seems there's a chap called Paramjit," said his friend Pappu to him one day as they sat on a tractor, chugging through fields of mustard. "On the other side of the river. Supposed to be a really good wrestler."

"How do you know?" asked Tarlochan.

"You know Manju chachi from Patiala? She told me," said Pappu. "But I told her very clearly that you were the best, hanji," he added quickly in case Tarlochan felt hurt.

Tarlochan, however, had other ideas. "How nice it would be to wrestle with him," he said. "Yes, that would be fun."

The following morning, Tarlochan slung a big bag of flour over his shoulder — a thousand kilos, can you imagine! — and set off to cross the river.

By the time he reached there, he was very thirsty and very hungry. So he sat down and made himself a hundred hot, hot rotis and drank up all the water in the river.

"Hrrraaaa!" came a loud trumpeting noise from behind Tarlochan. He turned around to see an elephant about to attack him. "This is my watering hole! You drank up all my water!" the elephant screamed angrily.

"Well, I am sorry ji," said Tarlochan.

But the elephant was upset and charged. Tarlochan simply stepped aside and picked it up by its tail. He balanced the elephant on his shoulders and crossed the river.

Tarlochan found Paramjit's house easily. "Oye Paramjitta! Are you home?" he called out.

"No bhaisaab, he's not," said his wife who opened the door. "He's gone to collect firewood."

"Changa, Bhabhi. Okay then, tell him Tarlochan from across the river wants to wrestle with him. Oh, I have a present for you," he said and threw the elephant into the courtyard.

'Mummmmeee!" came a thin, whining voice from inside. "Mummy, there's a mouse in the house!"

"It's an elephant, baby. Just sweep it away," said her mother. "And stop grumbling!"

Tarlochan shook his head. If the child thought the elephant was a mouse, what would the father be like? Hmmmm. . .

Tarlochan hummed under his breath. The eucalyptus trees made a cool, gentle breeze. Suddenly a cloud of dust began to grow and blow towards him. It grew bigger and blew thicker and out of the dust appeared big, burly Paramjit. He was pulling two hundred cartloads of firewood all by himself.

"Oye, brother Paramjitta!" said Tarlochan. "I've come to wrestle with you."

"Hey, I know you!" replied Paramjit. "You're that wrestler, Tarlochan Singh – from across the river. Oho! How I have wanted to meet you! Come, let's wrestle."

"That's exactly why I am here, brother! Are you ready?" exclaimed Tarlochan.

"Not here, not here, not here. Who's here to watch us? We are famous, Lochan-paaji, we need spectators," replied Paramjit.

"Oh haanji. Of course, of course," said Tarlochan. "So tell me, where will we find spectators?"

As Tarlochan and Paramjit scratched their heads and pondered on this matter, an old woman shuffled past. White curls peeped from underneath her bright pink dupatta.

"Biji! Biji!" Paramjit called to her. "Want to watch us wrestle? We're the biggest, the brightest, the best!"

"I'd love to, beta," the old woman replied. "Only, I have no time now. There that clever Jassu is running off with my camels. If I don't catch her I will lose them all, all hundred-and-fifty of them!"

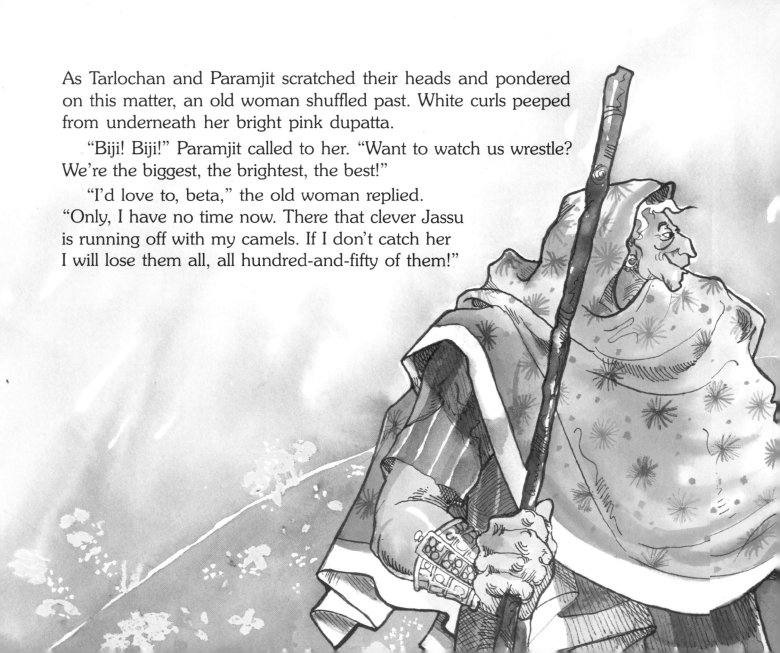

But when she saw how dejected the two looked, she thrust out her left hand and said, "Okay! Here, hop on to my palm. Then you can wrestle while I run and I can watch while you wrestle!"

"Great idea, Biji!" the two chorused and jumped onto the old woman's palm. In a second they began their bout and the old woman climbed slowly up a mountain.

There on the very top of another mountain, Jassu saw the old woman huff and puff her way up. "Oh no!" she exclaimed. "Looks like she's coming after me with an army!"

With a small shriek that made the trees jump out of their roots, she swept the camels onto a large red and green bedsheet, tied them up tight and ran with all her might, dragging the bundle behind her.

The camels squirmed and turned and tugged and hugged to find a comfortable corner on their bumpy bumpy ride. "Gudgudgudgudgud . . . gudgudgudgudgud . . ." groaned one camel. "Gudgudgudgudgud . . . gudgudgudgudgud . . ." moaned another.

"Oh shut up!" Jassu shouted. "So you are hungry now?" With another swipe she ripped out a farm full of apples and oranges and big green papayas and threw them into the bundle.

"Oye kudi! Girl, that's my farm you're making off with," yelled a farmer.

"Okay," said Jassu. "You come along too." She picked up the farmer and pushed him into the bundle. She stuffed in a couple of cows and goats too, for good measure, running all the time.

She stopped running only when she had reached the middle of a small town. In front stood a sweet shop. She barged in and demanded: "Some halwa-puri, quickly!"

"Only if you will pay," the mithaiwala replied.

"Huh!" said Jassu and with another great big swipe, sent him, his sweets, his shop, the whole town into the bedsheet which was bursting at its knots. Jassu started to run once more. Up the mountain she went and down again, up and down, up and down . . .

Jassu stopped only when she was so sleepy she couldn't take another step. She plucked a huge watermelon, made a slit in it and stuffed it with all the things in her bundle. She put the watermelon under her head to keep it safe and went to sleep.

Jassu slept and slept and slept.

While she slept, the skies darkened, the mountains trembled and swirling waters came down in a flood. Oh it was terrible! The swiftly flowing waters carried Jassu and her watermelon far far away.

When Jassu awoke after many many days, she found herself on an island surrounded by clear blue water. The sun shone high in the sky and all around were the things she had carried in her bundle: camels, trees, farmer, cows, sweet shop, mithaiwala, a little town . . .

All of them liked it so much they decided to live there, and Jassu even married the mithaiwala.

And what happened to the old woman? Well, she had given up the chase long ago because she just couldn't run any more. She sat under old, old Banyan on top of a hill, too tired to move. Suddenly she was surrounded by children of all sizes and shapes and colours. She was surprised. What was happening?

The children were looking at her left hand. She followed their gaze and laughed. "Oh, I completely forgot about you two fellows! No wonder my hand feels so heavy and stiff!" the old woman said. Tarlochan and Paramjit were still heaving and hustling on the palm of her left hand . . .

The old woman tossed them onto the ground where they continued to grip and grapple. "Come on, get him!," cried a small boy. "Oh, what a tackle, what a tackle!" exclaimed a small girl. There were shouts and cheers and clapping.

Slowly the old woman crawled her way out of the crowd. She took a few breaths of air, pulled the dupatta tight around her head, and went back the way she came. This time she walked.

Night fell and the children all went home only because they were hungry. Tarlochan and Paramjit wrestled and wrestled.

When the sun came up the next morning, the two big men lay on the ground snoring to glory, grunting and groaning in their sleep, and sometimes grabbing at the air with their hands.

There were no winners, no losers. Just a wish that came true for two young wrestlers from a land where women and men are strong and brave.

Balle! Balle!

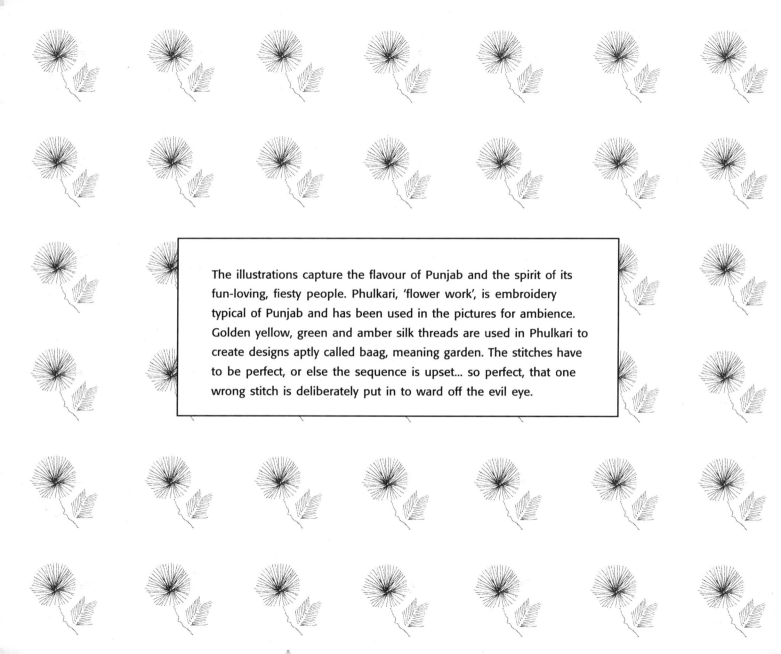

The illustrations capture the flavour of Punjab and the spirit of its fun-loving, fiesty people. Phulkari, 'flower work', is embroidery typical of Punjab and has been used in the pictures for ambience. Golden yellow, green and amber silk threads are used in Phulkari to create designs aptly called baag, meaning garden. The stitches have to be perfect, or else the sequence is upset... so perfect, that one wrong stitch is deliberately put in to ward off the evil eye.